·大喜說故事系列·

Tashi

and the
STOLEN CHILDREN

大喜與被擄走的小孩

Anna Fienberg　著
Barbara Fienberg

Kim Gamble　繪

王秋瑩　譯

三民書局

Jack **burst into** the kitchen. 'Tashi's back!' he cried.

'Oh, good,' said Dad. 'Has he been away?'
'Yes, I *told* you,' said Jack, 'don't you remember? He went back to the old country to see his grandmother for the New Year holiday. And while he was there, something terrible happened.'

傑克衝進了廚房，大聲喊著：「大喜回來了！」

　　「喔！好啊！」老爸說。「他有出門去嗎？」

　　「我告訴過你的，」傑克說，「你不記得了啦？他回老家去陪他奶奶過新年啊！而且啊，就在那裡，發生了可怕的事情喲！」

burst into...　衝進…；闖入…

'His grandmother ran away with the circus?' suggested Dad.

'No,' said Jack. 'She can't **juggle**. But listen, you know the war lord who came looking for Tashi last year?'

'Yes, I do remember him,' said Dad. 'He was the only war lord in Wilson Street last summer, so I won't forget him **in a hurry**.'

'Yes, and guess what,' Jack began, but Mum **interrupted** him.

「他奶奶跟馬戲團跑了？」老爸說。

「不是的，」傑克說，「她又不會雜耍。不過，你們記得去年來找大喜的那個督軍吧？」

「是啊！我記得他，」爸爸說，「他是去年夏天威爾森街唯一的督軍，所以我不會那麼快就忘記他的。」

「那好，猜一猜，」傑克開始要說了，不過老媽打斷了他。

juggle [`dʒʌgl̩] 動 雜耍
in a hurry 輕易地；匆匆忙忙
interrupt [ˌɪntəˈrʌpt] 動 打斷

'Come and have some afternoon tea, while you tell us,' she said, and brought a tray into the living room.

'Well,' said Jack, when they were settled comfortably. 'It was like this. When Tashi arrived back in his village, it was all quiet. *Strangely* quiet. None of his old friends were playing in the **square**, and he could hear someone crying.

「來喝個下午茶，再一邊告訴我們吧！」老媽說著，把茶盤端進了客廳。

　　「嗯！」當大夥兒舒舒服服地坐好的時候，傑克開始說了，「事情是這樣的。大喜回到村子的時候，一切都好安靜，出奇地安靜。沒有一個老朋友在廣場上玩，可是他聽見有人在哭。

square [skwɛr] 名 廣場

His grandfather told him that the war lord had just made a **raid** through the village. He'd **captured** nearly all the young men for his **army**—and he had **kidnapped** six children **as well**!'

他爺爺告訴他說那個督軍剛襲擊過村子，全村的男子幾乎都被他抓去充軍，他還擄走了六個小孩呢！」

raid [red] 名 突擊

capture [`kæptʃɚ] 動 俘虜

army [`ɑrmɪ] 名 軍隊

kidnap [`kɪdnæp] 動 綁架

as well 也（＝too）

'**What** did he take the *children* **for**?' asked Mum.
'So that the men would fight **bravely** and not
run away home,' Jack told her. 'If they didn't
fight, he was going to **punish** the children.'
'He **deserves** to be fried in a fritter, that war
lord!' exploded Dad.

「他抓這些孩童要做什麼？」老媽問。

「這樣這些男人才會勇敢地打仗，不會逃跑回家。」傑克告訴她說。「要是他們不打仗，督軍便會懲罰這些小孩。」

「那個督軍真該下油鍋哪！」爸爸大聲說。

what...for? 為什麼…？
bravely [`brevlɪ] 副 勇敢地
punish [`pʌnɪʃ] 動 懲罰
deserve [dɪ`zɝv] 動 應受（獎賞，處罰）

'Yes,' agreed Jack. 'Well, just then the Wan twins came running back into the village square.

'They had hidden while the **soldiers seized** the young men. Then they'd followed the war party to see where their uncles were being taken.

「對呀！」傑克附和著。「嗯！就在那時候，王家雙胞胎跑回村子的廣場。

　　「在士兵動手抓年輕人的時候，他們躲了起來，然後跟著兵團去瞧瞧他們的叔叔被帶到那兒。

soldier [`soldʒɚ] 图 士兵

seize [siz] 勔 抓住

'The twins said that the children had been put in the **dungeon** of the war lord's **palace**. The twins searched and climbed and tapped and dug, but they could find no way in. They said the children were lost forever.

「雙胞胎倆說這些小孩被關到督軍皇宮的地牢裡。他們用盡了各種方法，都沒法兒找到入口。他們還說那些小孩要永遠消失了。

dungeon [`dʌndʒən] 名 地牢
palace [`pæləs] 名 宮殿

'Everybody in the square listened to the Wan twins' story, and a **dreadful moaning** began. The sound of sadness rose and swelled like a wave. Parents and aunties and cousins hung onto each other **as if** they were **drowning**. Then, one by one, people turned to Tashi. He had once worked for the war lord in that very palace.'

「廣場上的村民聽著王家雙胞胎敘述經過，不禁悲傷地歎起氣來。哀傷的聲音如浪潮般響起。這些小孩的父母、叔叔、阿姨像溺水般緊緊相擁在一起。接著，村民紛紛轉向大喜，因為他曾經在督軍的那座皇宮裡工作過。」

dreadful [ˋdrɛdfəl] 形 可怕的
moan [mon] 動 哀嘆
as if 宛如
drown [draʊn] 動 溺水

'Uh oh,' Dad shook his head. 'I bet he was wishing that he had gone on holidays another time.'

'Not Tashi,' said Jack. 'He slipped away to think, and when he returned he went to his grandfather's box of firecrackers and filled his pockets. Then he set off for the palace of the war lord.

By evening, he reached the field where the soldiers were **camped**.

「喔！喔！」老爸搖搖頭。「我敢打賭大喜一定希望改天能有機會去渡假的。」

　　「大喜沒有。」傑克說。「大喜溜開去想了想，他回來後，便到爺爺的鞭炮箱裡拿鞭炮裝滿口袋，然後就往督軍的皇宮出發。在黃昏前他便到達了士兵紮營的營地。

camp [kæmp] 動 搭帳篷

'He crept past the guards and found the uncles. They were miserable, sitting silent and cold, far from the cooking fires. Tashi whispered to them that they must get ready to leave at any moment, as he was on his way to the dungeon. One man clung to him, crying, "My little sister is only five years old, Tashi. She will be so frightened. You must find the children." Tashi **promised** to be back by morning.

「他躡手躡腳地穿過衛兵，找到叔叔們。他們靜靜地坐在離營火遠遠的地方，又冷又可憐。大喜一邊低聲要他們作好隨時離開的準備，一邊往地窖前進。有個人緊緊抓住他不放，哭喊著說：『我的小妹妹只有五歲大，她一定害怕極了。你得找到這些小孩啊！』大喜答應明早前一定會回來。

promise [ˋprɑmɪs] 動 允諾

'Then he went on alone. He remembered a secret passage into the palace that he'd **discovered** when he was living there before. You entered in a cave nearby and came out through a wardrobe in the war lord's very own bedroom.'

'Ugh,' **shuddered** Mum. 'I'd rather be anywhere in the world than *there*.'

'I know,' shivered Dad. 'A man like that, you can imagine how his socks smell.'

「然後他繼續一個人往前走。他記得以前住在這裡的時候，曾發現一條通往皇宮的秘密通道。走進附近的一個洞穴後，便會從督軍臥室的衣櫃出來。」

　　「哎呀！」老媽嚇得發抖。「我寧可在世界上的任何地方，也不願在那裡！」

　　「我了解。」老爸也發起抖來。「像那種人，也就不難想像他的襪子有多臭了！」

discover [dɪ`skʌvɚ] 動 發現
shudder [`ʃʌdɚ] 動 顫抖

'Well, anyway,' Jack went on, 'Tashi found the cave and pulled aside the bushes covering the **entrance**. He ran through the damp tunnel and **held his breath** as he pushed at the wardrobe door. It creaked. What if the war lord had just come upstairs to get a sharper sword?'

'Or change his socks?' put in Dad.

「不管怎樣，」傑克接著說，「大喜找到了那個洞穴，他撥開蓋住入口的草叢，快步跑過潮溼的隧道，就在他要推開衣櫃門的時候，他摒住了呼吸。門嘎吱一聲開了。如果這時督軍跑上樓來拿利劍的話該怎麼辦呢？」

　　「或是換襪子？」老爸插嘴說。

entrance [`ɛntrəns] 名 入口
hold one's breath 停止呼吸

'Tashi held his breath. He **peeped** around the door. The room was empty. He **tiptoed** out into the hall and down the stairs. At the last step he stopped. He felt the firecrackers in his pockets, and **quivered**. A daring plan had popped into his head. But, he wondered, was he brave enough to do it?

「大喜摒住呼吸，從門縫中偷偷往外瞧。房間裡面空無一人。他躡手躡腳地走進大廳，下了樓。他在最後一個階梯停了下來，他摸摸口袋裡的鞭炮，全身顫抖著。一個大膽的計畫閃過他的腦海，不過他很懷疑自己夠不夠勇敢這麼做？

peep [pip] 勔 從縫中偷看

tiptoe [`tɪpˌto] 勔 踮腳走路

quiver [`kwɪvɚ] 勔 顫抖

'Instead of going further down the stairs into the dungeon, he found his way along to the kitchens. The cooks were busy preparing a grand dinner for the war lord and didn't notice Tashi as he crawled behind the oil jars and around the rice bins.'

'What was he doing?' asked Mum.

'Having a little **snack,** of course,' said Dad, taking a bite of Jack's scone.

「他沒有繼續下樓到地窖去，而是走到廚房。廚師們正忙著為督軍準備豐盛的晚餐，根本沒注意到大喜已經悄悄來到油罐後面，躲在米箱堆中。」

　　「他在做什麼啊？」老媽問。

　　「當然是吃些點心囉！」老爸邊說，邊咬了一口傑克的鬆餅。

snack [snæk] 名 點心

'You'll find out if you **pay attention**,' said Jack, and he moved his scone to the other hand. 'When Tashi left the kitchen he could hear the cries of the children, and the sound of their sobbing led him down to the dungeon. Two guards were talking outside the dark, barred room where the children were held. Tashi **hopped** into an empty barrel close by and called out in a great loud voice, *"The war lord is a beetle-brain!"*'

「如果你專心聽的話，便會知道究竟的。」傑克説著，把鬆餅換到另一隻手上。

　　「大喜離開廚房時，有聽到孩子們的哭鬧聲，他順著這個聲音來到了下面的地窖。兩名衛兵守在那關著小孩的暗牢外頭。大喜跳進旁邊的一個空桶子，然後大叫一聲：『督軍是個大笨蛋！』」

pay attention　注意傾聽

hop [hɑp]　動 跳

'*NO!*' cried Mum and Dad together.

'*YES!*' **crowed** Jack. 'The guards jumped as if they'd just sat on a nest of **soldier ants**. "One of those **pesky** children has managed to get out!" the fat guard hissed. "Then we'd better catch him," said the other, "before the war lord boils us in spider sauce."

'As soon as they ran off, Tashi turned the big key they had left in the lock and opened the dungeon door.

「不好了！」爸媽異口同聲地說。

「才不呢！」傑克得意極了。「那衛兵就像坐在兵蟻穴上般地跳了起來。『有個麻煩的小鬼偷溜出去了！』胖胖的那名衛兵咒罵著。『那麼我們最好在督軍把我們丟到蜘蛛湯裡煮以前，把他抓回來！』另一名衛兵說。

「他們一跑開，大喜馬上就轉動他們留在鎖上的大鑰匙，打開了地窖的門。

crow [kro] 動 歡呼

soldier ant 兵蟻

pesky [`pɛskɪ] 形 麻煩的

'The children **recognized** Tashi and crowded around, telling him all that had happened. "Shush," whispered Tashi, "wait till we get outside. The danger isn't over yet."

「小孩認出是大喜，都圍了過來，告訴他事情發生的經過。『噓！』大喜低聲說，『到外頭再說吧！還很危險哪！」

recognize [ˋrɛkəɡˌnaɪz] 勔 認出

'He led them quickly up the stairs and through the long hallways until at last they came to the great wooden front door of the palace. Tashi reached up and pulled on the big brass latch. The door **swung** open and the children whooped with joy. They **streamed** out, falling over each other in their hurry. Tashi picked up the littlest one and set him on his feet. "Home we go!" he cried.

「大喜帶領他們迅速上樓，穿過長長的走廊，終於來到皇宮巨大的木板前門。大喜搆了上去，用力拉動大銅鎖。門打開了，孩子們高興地大叫起來。他們蜂湧而出，匆忙間還互相絆倒。大喜拉起了最小的小孩，催促他趕快，『我們回家吧！』他喊著。

swing [swɪŋ] 動 轉動成某狀態
（過去式 swung [swʌŋ]）
stream [strim] 動 流動

'But no. Just then a huge hand reached down and **plucked** Tashi up by the collar. He was face to face with the **furious** war lord. Their noses almost touched. The war lord's skin was rough, like sandpaper.

"*RUN!*" Tashi called to the children. "Run to your uncles down by the camp!"

「不過事情沒這麼順利。就在這個時候，一隻巨大的手伸了下來，拎起大喜的領子，將大喜提在半空中。大喜和那憤怒的督軍臉對著臉，鼻子幾乎都要湊在一起了。督軍的皮膚像砂紙一般粗糙。

　　「『快跑！』大喜對著孩子們大叫。『快跑到下面軍營那邊找你們的叔叔吧！』

pluck [plʌk] 動 拉

furious [`fjʊrɪəs] 形 憤怒的

'The war lord shook Tashi, as if he were a scrap of dirty washing. His iron **knuckles** bit into Tashi's neck. He breathed fish and grease into Tashi's face. "So, you foolish boy," he growled. "You have come back. You won't escape again. Look well at the daylight outside, for this is the last time you'll see it. You'll work in the dungeons **from now on**."

「大喜就像一小塊髒衣服般被督軍搖來晃去。督軍那鐵一般的手指節掐進大喜的脖子，腥騷的氣息噴到大喜的臉上。他咆哮著：『哈！你這笨小孩，又回來了啊！這次你可逃不掉了。好好欣賞外頭的陽光吧！因為這是你最後一次看到太陽了，從現在起你就到地牢裡去幹活吧！』

knuckle [ˋnʌkl̩] 名 指關節
from now on　今後

'Tashi thought of the **mean** black bars on the window of the dungeon. Only a cockroach could stay alive in there. His eyes began to water and he started to **sniff**.

'"Scared, are you?" the war lord **jeered**.
'"No, I can smell something,"
said Tashi, "can't you?"'
'Socks!' cried Dad.

「大喜想到地牢窗戶上那醜陋陰暗的柵欄，恐怕只有蟑螂才能在那裡生存吧！他的眼眶溼了起來，不禁吸了吸鼻子。

　　『『害怕了，是不是？』督軍嘲笑著。

　　『『不是，我聞到什麼味道，』大喜說，『你沒聞到嗎？』』

　　「臭襪子！」老爸大叫。

mean [min] 形 醜陋的

sniff [snɪf] 動 抽鼻子

jeer [dʒɪr] 動 冷笑

'The war lord sniffed. The air *did* seem rather smoky. Suddenly there was a loud **explosion** and they heard feet pounding over the stone floor. "Fire!" shouted the war lord, and he dropped Tashi and ran off towards the noise, calling for the guards to follow him.

「督軍聞了聞，空氣中真的好像有煙味。突然間一聲巨大的爆炸聲響起，接著他們聽到劈劈啪啪踩過石頭地面的腳步聲。『失火了！』督軍大叫一聲，丟下大喜，轉身便往喧鬧的地方跑去，還一面呼叫衛兵跟隨他。

explosion [ɪk`sploʒən] 名 爆炸（聲）

'Tashi sped down the steps and soon found the children and their uncles. They were waiting for him over the hill, beyond the camp. From there they had a good **view** of the palace.

'It was **blazing fiercely**—the windows were red with the glow of fire inside, and a great grey cloud of smoke climbed above it.

「大喜迅速地跑下階梯，一會兒便找到小孩以及他們的叔叔。大夥兒在軍營外的山頭等著他，從這裡可以把皇宮看得一清二楚。

view [vju] 名 景色

火勢燃燒猛烈——裡頭熾熱的火燄照得窗戶一片通紅，陣陣濃密的煙霧竄了出來。

blaze [blez] 動 熊熊燃燒

fiercely [`fɪrslɪ] 副 猛烈地

'"Weren't we lucky the fire started just then!" said the littlest boy. His brother laughed and looked at Tashi. "I don't think luck **had anything to do with** it." he said.

'"Well," said Tashi **modestly, "as a matter of fact** I did empty the gunpowder out of my firecrackers and laid a trail up to the kitchen stove. I hoped we would manage to get out before it reached the ovens. It **blew up** just **in time**."

『『我們可真幸運哪！火正好這時候燒起來。』那個最小的男孩說。他哥哥笑著看看大喜說：『我可不認為這有什麼幸不幸運的。』

　　『嗯！』大喜謙虛地說，『事實上是我把帶來的鞭炮火藥倒出來，接上一條引線到廚房的火爐，我是希望我們能在引線燒到火爐前逃脫。火藥引爆得真是時候哪！』

have something to do with... 與…有關係

modestly [`mɑdɪstlɪ] 副 謙虛地

as a matter of fact 事實上（=in fact）

blow up 爆炸

in time 及時

'"What a clever Tashi!" the children **yelled**, and the uncles **hoisted** him up onto their shoulders and they sang and danced all the way home.

'Phew!' said Dad. 'That was a close shave. I suppose Tashi could **relax** after that, and enjoy the rest of his holiday. Did he have good weather?'

「『大喜好聰明喲!』孩子們歡呼了起來,然後叔叔們把他們扛在肩上,一路上邊唱歌邊跳舞地回家。」

　　「呼!」老爸鬆了一口氣,「可說是僥倖脫險啊!我想大喜在那事件後可以好好地休息,享受剩餘的假期了吧!那他心情好嗎?」

yell [jɛl] 動 叫喊

hoist [hɔɪst] 動 舉起

relax [rɪ`læks] 動 放鬆

'Yes, at first,' said Jack, 'until the witch, Baba Yaga, blew in on the winds of a dreadful storm.'
'Baba Yaga?' said Dad **nervously**. 'Who is she?'
'Oh, just a witch whose **favorite** meal is baked children. But Tashi will tell us all about that. What's for dinner tonight, Mum?'

「剛開始的時候好啊！」傑克說，「直到巫婆巴巴鴉加刮起了可怕的狂風暴雨。」

「巴巴鴉加？」老爸緊張地問。「她是誰呀？」

「噢！她是個最喜歡烤小孩來吃的巫婆。大喜會把一切告訴我們的，媽，今天晚上吃什麼呀？」

nervously [`nɝvəslɪ] 副 緊張地
favorite [`fevrɪt] 形 最喜愛的

小普羅藝術叢書

·小畫家的天空系列·

活用不同的創作工具

靈活表現各種題材

讓青少年朋友動手又動腦

創造一個夢想的世界

國家圖書館出版品預行編目資料

大喜與被擄走的小孩 / Anna Fienberg,Barbara Fien-
berg著;Kim Gamble繪;王秋瑩譯.－－初版一刷.－
－臺北市；三民，民90
　　面;公分--(探索英文叢書.大喜說故事系列;8)
中英對照
ISBN 957-14-3418-3 　(平裝)
　1. 英國語言－讀本

805.18　　　　　　　　　　　　　　　90002915

網路書店位址　http://www.sanmin.com.tw

© 　大喜與被擄走的小孩

著作人　Anna Fienberg　Barbara Fienberg
繪　圖　Kim Gamble
譯　者　王秋瑩
發行人　劉振強
著作財　三民書局股份有限公司
產權人　臺北市復興北路三八六號
發行所　三民書局股份有限公司
　　　　地址／臺北市復興北路三八六號
　　　　電話／二五〇〇六六〇〇
　　　　郵撥／〇〇〇九九九八——五號
印刷所　三民書局股份有限公司
門市部　復北店／臺北市復興北路三八六號
　　　　重南店／臺北市重慶南路一段六十一號
初版一刷　中華民國九十年四月
編　號　S 85586
定　價　新臺幣壹佰柒拾元
行政院新聞局登記證局版臺業字第〇二〇〇號

ISBN　957-14-3418-3　(平裝)